Blue Canyon Horse

Also by Ann Nolan Clark

Blue Canyon Horse

BY ANN NOLAN CLARK

ILLUSTRATED BY ALLAN HOUSER

The Viking Press

NEW YORK

Lithographed in U.S.A. by DUENEWALD·KONECKY·LITHOGRAPHERS, INC.

Blue Canyon Horse

In lush green fields beside blue water
  a little mare is feeding,
  swishing her tail in calm delight
  and feeding.

The night is still.
The stars above are far away.
The night winds hush the noisy waters.
The canyon is shadow-filled and still.

The little mare stops feeding,
　　stops to listen, to whinny,
　　to listen . . . .
Something wild is calling in the night time.
It is calling in the shadows.
It is calling through the canyon.

The wild call is the call of freedom.
It is the call of the wild herds.
It is the call of instinct.

The little mare listens
　　and, listening, trembles.

She runs
   like the wind before the storm,
   like the gray mist before the dawn,
   like the cold before the sun.

She runs,
   trampling the wet green of the fields,
   splashing the blue water of the river,
   clattering the loose stones on the trail.

She runs. She runs.

Cliffs, where the mescals bloom, rise upward,
   pink-red and purple-blue,
   violet and rose.
Cliffs, where the cacti bloom, rise upward
   from the floor of the canyon,
   from the heart of the world.
The trail is narrow and steep.
The little horse stumbles,
   climbing upward.

The trail is a zigzag wound
  on the canyon wall.
The little mare halts
  to fight for breath,
  to rest, to listen,
  heaving, trembling,
  faltering.

Sharp stones cut her feet.
Cactus spines pierce her hocks.
The little horse stumbles,
  climbing upward.

12

Far below on the canyon floor
   a blue river flows
   by the cottonwood trees,
   by the peach and the fig trees,
   by the purple grapevines,
   by the green alfalfa,
   by the Indian shelters and the campfires.
The horse looks down
   on the sleeping canyon
   at the foot of the trail.

The horse looks down
    on the sleeping canyon
    at the foot of the trail.
There lie shelter and food.
There lie comfort and safety.
There lies friendship
    with the boy, her master.
There below, at the foot of the trail,
    lies the world she has known.

Then the wild urge
    like the sting of the whiplash flicks her.
Her nostrils flare. She whirls,
    turning from the known world
    to answer the call of the wild unknown.

The still night passes to make way
    for the whispering dawn.

The horse is gone.
The field is empty.

Only an echo in the wind,
    only a hoofprint on the trail,
    to tell the boy who owns her,
    who calls to her,
    who searches for her,
    that here, last night,
    a horse passed by.

15

The day grows into noon
    and lengthens into evening.

Night comes,
    lonely and long,
    for the Indian boy
    whose horse has gone.
Sleep does not come
    to heal his hurt.
Dreams do not come
    to kindle hope.
His horse has gone.

The little horse reaches
    the level mesa top.
She roams restlessly,
    nibbling the bunch grass,
    drinking the rain pools,
    sleeping ... uneasy ...
    waking ... uncertain ...
    searching for something.

At night the little horse runs,
  runs in the wind,
  runs in the darkness,
  answering the call
  of the wild unknown.

In a mountain meadow,
    among the pines of the high places,
    a herd of wild horses is feeding,
    kicking and biting, nickering and calling,
    free as the clouds above them,
    free as the land around them,
    free as the rain and the wind and the stars.

The little mare watches them.
She watches the wild herd
    led by the mare leader,
    guarded by the herd sire,
    the Chieftain.

She watches them,
    afraid but curious, fearful but excited,
    not understanding, not knowing,
    guided by instinct alone,
    hiding and watching, and at last joining
    the herd of wild horses.

Then comes midsummer
  to canyon and valley,
  to mesa and meadow.

The sun comes close to the mountains.
Its warmth melts the snow on the peaks
  and the fears from the hearts of the wild
      things.

The deer and the elk stop feeding
  to watch the wild horses run in the wind.
The fawns stop their gentle play
  while the wild colts run through the aspen.

On the floor of the canyon
   the apricots ripen,
   and the corn,
   and the peaches.

The boy works
   in the fields
   and the gardens
   but his heart
   is not with him.

His heart roams the mesa
   at the top of the canyon.
His heart calls the horse
   that he has cared for
   and tended.

In the meadows the horse herd roams,
    and on the mountaintops.
In the valleys the horse herd roams,
    and on the high mesas.
The little mare is with them.

Her sides are sleek with the fat of summer.
Her mane is thick like a stormcloud blowing.
The wild wind is in her feet
    and in her blood.
She knows no master.

At the campfires at night
   the Indian young men
   talk to the boy,
   to their young brother.

"She is with the wild herd,"
   they tell him.
"We have seen her.
We know it.
Let us all ride together
   and surround her
   and trap her."

The boy answers them,
   "No.
      If she comes back
         by herself,
         I will know
         she is mine."

Moon-of-Little-Rains comes,
  and Moon-of-Summer-Storms.

The thunders roll.
The lightnings flash.
The rains pour down.

The little horse is one with them,
  and one with the wild herd running.

At the campfires at night
   the Indian old men
   talk to the boy,
   to the child of their People.

"The heart of the little mare,"
   they tell him,
   "is wild and free,
   as our hearts
   would be wild and free
   if the years
   had not taught us
   that the price
   of too much freedom
   is pain."

The boy does not answer.

It is the time of the Mesquite-Moon,
    when the mesquite pods and the sunflowers,
    the fruits and the corn plants,
    the pumpkins and the piñons,
    have ripened in harvest.

The wild horse herd comes down from the
        mountains
    to the mesa top
    to feed on the seed-heavy wild grass,
    to drowse in the sun-filled noons,
    and to flee in playful terror
    before the frost winds of autumn.

On the floor of the canyon
   the corn is harvested.
The cactus fruit is cut.
The piñon nuts are gathered.
The storerooms of the People
   are full
   of food
   for the winter.
Snow fills the canyon.
The boy's heart is bleak.
His little horse is gone.

The little mare leads the wild herd,
    her tail and mane streaming backward,
    her nostrils quivering against the wind.
Gone is fear from her heart,
    gone is the knowledge of sheltered living.

She leads the wild horses.
Proudly the herd sire,
    the fleet-footed stallion,
    brings up the rear
    to protect the weak ones,
    to nip at the stragglers.
Proudly he runs with the herd,
    and the little mare leads them.

She is scarred and unshod,
    burr-matted and rough-coated,
    but she is beautiful
    because she is free.

Snow peak and grassland,
    storm and stars and wind and rain,
    she is part of them.
She has no master.

The little mare leads the wild herd.
She is the favorite. She is the leader,
   wise and courageous, fleet-footed and
      fearless.
She leads the horses from danger
   when man would capture them
   with ropes and gate traps.
She leads the horses from danger
   when man would ride them down
   to end their freedom.
She leads the horses around
   the slide slopes and the swamps.
She is the first to scent danger,
   to see the crouching form,
   to hear the padded footfall.
She is first and fastest. She is leader.

Moon-of-the-Harvest is over
  with its fruitful giving.

Thunder closes its house doors against the
    cold.
Lightning folds in upon itself to sleep.

Frost paints the leaves of the cottonwood
      trees.
Wind beckons them, teases them, coaxes them
      to go dancing.

Snowclouds gather in the house of the
      mountains,
  veiling the peaks from the world below.

The deer and the antelope come down from
      the mountains
  to the mesa top,
  to eat the mesquite pods and the wild grass.

Snow-Moon comes with its threat of snow.

Snow falls and drifts
   and melts and freezes
   and falls anew.
Snow falls, hiding the days.
Snow falls, hiding the nights.
Time stands still.

There is no movement but the falling snow.
There is no sound but the falling snow.
There is little food. There is no warmth.
Time stands still.

On the mesa top
   the wild horses stand with bowed heads.
They stand snow-covered, ghostlike and cold.

On the floor of the canyon
   the boy stands alone
   in the snow-covered field.
Time stands still.

The storm breaks. The moon lights the world.
The horses paw through the frozen snow
   for the tender blades of grass to eat.

The little mare paws the snow,
   then stops to listen.

Something is calling, faintly.
Something is stirring, dimly.
Is it a memory of other ways of life?
Is it a longing for other ways of living?

Coyotes howl in the moonlight,
   and the horses flee
   over the hard-crusted snow.
The little mare leads them.

Gone is the memory of other ways of living.
Gone is the longing for another way of life.
The wild herd is wild,
   and wild is the lead mare,
   wild and free.

38

The storms break, but the snow stays on.
Too long it stays.
The world is weary with its heaviness.

The wild horses grow gaunt and lean.
Their coats are dull.
Their eyes are hunted-looking.
Beasts of prey stalk them.
Hunger stalks them. Death stalks them.

They flounder in the snowdrifts,
    weakened from cold,
    the need for food,
    and fear.

Slowly the world shakes itself of winter
    and welcomes the time of the Planting-
        Moon.

The little mare grows restless. She feels strange.
She knows not why. She does not reason.
She has only instinct.

She looks down into the canyon.
It seems to draw her into its keeping.
Is it someplace she has known?
Is there a familiar scent on the wind?
Is there someone waiting in the canyon?

At the foot of the trail there is shelter.
There is safety better than fleetness.
There is friendship better than freedom.
Instinct tells her to go down.

On the mesa top at the head of the trail,
   by the mesquite and the cacti,
   where the mescal blooms,
   the little mare rests.
The herd sire guards her.

On the mesa top at the head of the trail,
   by the mesquite and the cacti,
   where the mescal blooms,
   her colt is born.

The little mare's colt is born
   by the light of the Mescal-Moon.

Mothered by the green fields,
   fathered in the wastelands,
   the little colt is born.

The little colt is born.

In the canyon below
   the boy sleeps
   and dreams.
The dream is misted,
   unreal,
   unfinished,
   but in it flickers
   a spark of hope.

High on the trail of the colored cliffs
   the little mare walks proudly, nosing her
      colt.
She has remembered the fields by the river.
She has remembered the boy who was master.
She is going home with her baby.

Gone is the feeling of wildness and flight.
Gone is the need for the mountain peak.
Gone is the love for the wild herd fleeing.
Home is the place for her baby.

The little mare steps proudly.
She arches her neck. She whinnies softly.
She swings along, nosing and nudging
   her long-legged colt.
She is going home with her baby.

Strong are her feelings for the need of shelter,
   for the need of kindness and the love of a
      master.
She now knows something that is better than
      freedom.
She is taking her baby home.

46

The boy is restless.
He is uneasy.
He begins to climb
    the mesa trail,
    taking his hunting bow.

47

The little mare steps proudly down the trail.
Far below she sees the green of the fields
   and the blue of the river.
But wait—there is danger on the trail.
There is a scent on the wind.

The little mare shivers in terror.
She pushes her colt against the cliff
   to shelter it from the enemy.
She turns to face the foe.
A tawny form crouches among the mescal.
A lean yellow form springs from the rock
      ledge,
   slashing the mare's breast
   with its great claws.
The little mare screams.
She screams in pain for herself
   and in terror for her colt.
Then from the trail an arrow flies
   straight to its mark—
   a lion scream—a spurt of blood—
   the great beast slithers from the cliff wall
   to the floor of the canyon below.

The Indian boy runs up the trail
   to kneel by the side of the wounded horse.
The little mare looks up at him.
She knows him.
She is glad to see him.
She has not forgotten.
He is her master.
She is safe with him.
Her baby is safe.

High in the sky the buzzards circle.
There is blood on the trail.
There is death in the canyon.

But against the cliff
  there is sound of the living.
There is movement of life
  as the little mare rises
  to nuzzle her colt.

The Indian boy comes to them,
  his eyes clear of fear.

Death cannot touch them now.
He is with them.
His mare knows
  that he is her master.
His mare knows
  that he will take her
  and her baby home.

In lush green fields beside blue waters
   the mare and her colt are feeding.

The night is still.
The stars above are far away.
The night winds hush the noisy waters.
The canyon is shadow-filled and still.

Gone is the wild urge
   like the sting of a whiplash.
Gone is the wild call
   from the top of the mesa.

The mare looks around
   at the sleeping canyon
   by the foot of the trail.
Here are shelter and food.
Here are comfort and safety.
Here is friendship
   with the boy, her master.
Here below, at the foot of the trail,
   is the world she knows.

She is home.

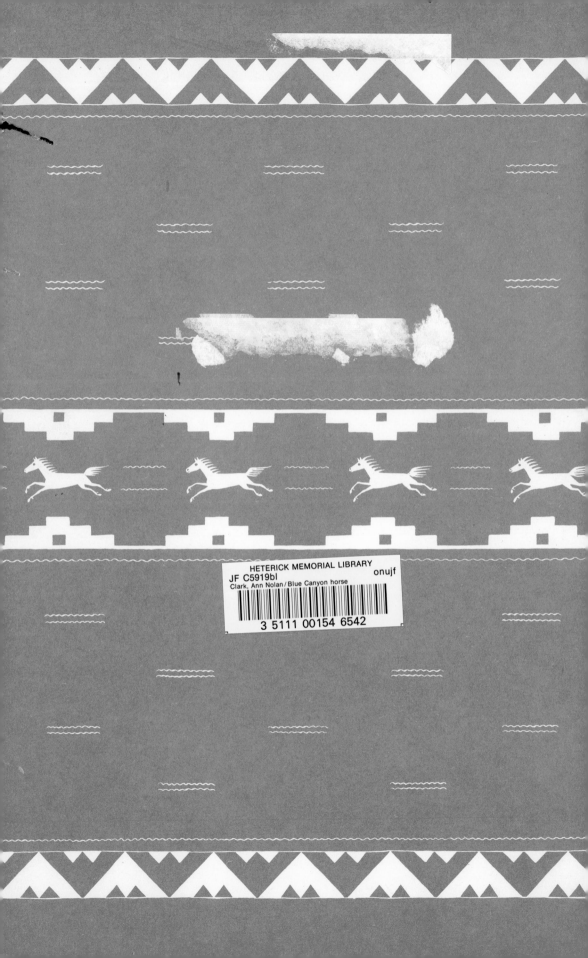